Slimy Snail set out on a trail
one bright and sunny morning.

He went up a hill,
it was very steep –

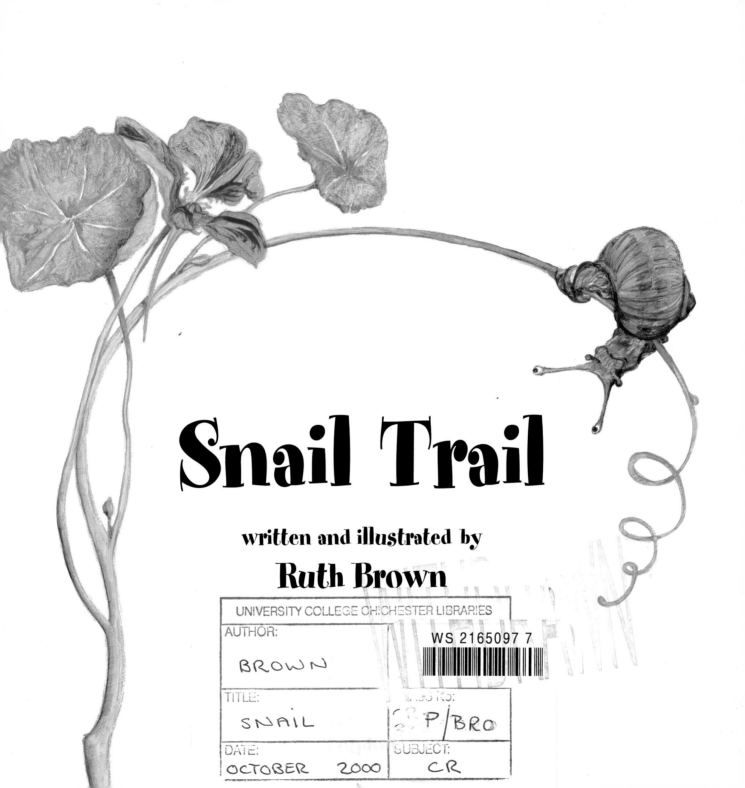

Snail Trail

written and illustrated by
Ruth Brown

through a tunnel,
very gloomy –

into a forest,
very quiet –

over a bridge,
very high –

down a slope,
very slippery –

up to an arch,
very narrow –

past some flowers,
very pretty –

and into a dark, dark cave.

He curled up in his shell,
very small –

and was very soon
asleep.